THE SEASONS

Spring

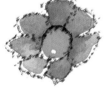

BARRON'S

D1511887

Winter is coming to an end, snow starts to melt, and almond trees *bloom.*
It is springtime!

The weather is a little crazy: it is sunny, it rains, sometimes it even hails … and then a *rainbow* appears in the sky. Can you count how many colors it has?

The sun rises earlier and sets a little later. It gets warmer and warmer. What *time* do you go to school? What time do you get off?

Flowers

appear everywhere
and trees grow leaves
again. Everything is
full of color.
What color are all
these flowers?

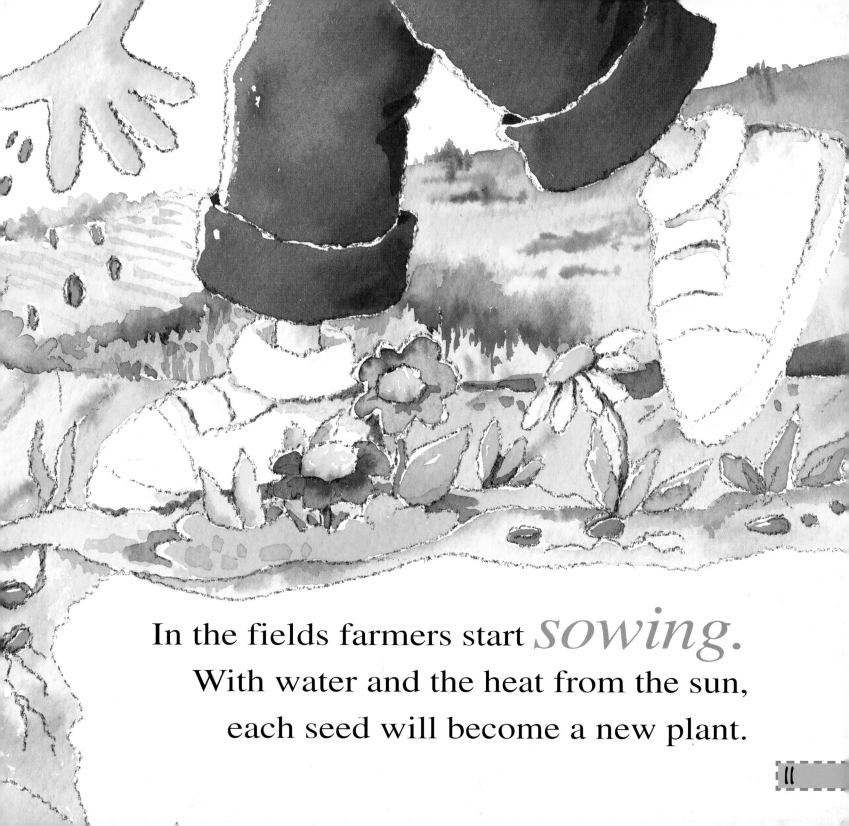

In the fields farmers start *sowing.*
With water and the heat from the sun,
each seed will become a new plant.

Swallows come back looking for the *nests* they abandoned in the fall.

Do you know what the nests
are made of?

On the farm many *animals* are born and they follow their mothers everywhere. Some come from their mother's belly and others are born from an egg.

See if you can guess how these little animals were born.

Ponds are full of tadpoles just out of the egg. A few weeks later they will become proud *frogs.*

Help them find flies to eat.

Bees love spring; they fly from flower to flower and they make delicious honey with the nectar they pick up!

How many legs do they have?

18

The sun is warm,
there is a nice soft
breeze …
let's *play*
outside !

There are special holidays in the spring, such as Easter. How many hidden *eggs* can you find?

24

It is time to take care of *plants* at home, at the park … and also to rearrange your closet; you have outgrown your clothes from last year for sure!

Fields and gardens are full of
vegetables and fruits:
watermelons, red currants, radishes…

Can you recognize any others?

How about taking an excursion into the woods? You may find many different *insects* there ! Spring is great !

Easter ring

Shall we make an Easter ring to decorate a corner at home or at school? A nice bunny can keep you company during the Easter season.

You just need cardboard in different colors.

1. Trace the ring and the little flowers and cut them out with the help of an adult. The ring will look nicer if you make little drawings on it.

2. Trace the bunny and cut out its figure. You may use some colored cardboard or a white one and then paint the bunny.

3. Glue the lower part of the bunny, indicated by the dotted line, to the ring and the two little flowers as shown in the illustration.

Finally, make a little hole at the top of the ring,

and pass a piece of string through it to hang it.

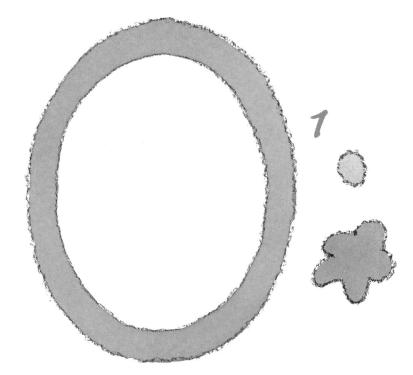

A plant is born

Plants are born from seeds. First the seed falls on the ground and later it is covered by soil. The seed then opens and a little root comes out, as well as a stem with tiny leaves. The root grows downward and the stem upward and more leaves sprout from it. Would you like to see how it works?

Get a few lentils, wrap them in damp cotton and put everything in a transparent container. Place it where there is plenty of indirect natural daylight and wait.

After a few days you will see that little plants start to grow.

A paper frog

How about making a few frogs? Here is an idea. You just need a square piece of colored paper and to follow the instructions.

Find a dry leaf and glue the frog on top!

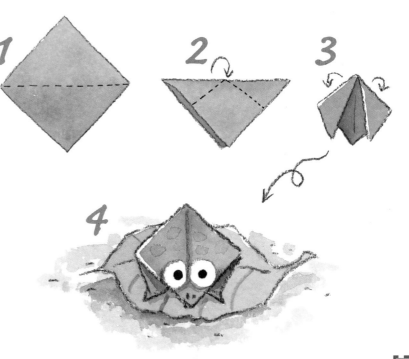

Let's make paper eggs!

Draw as many eggs as you want on pieces of cardboard in different colors. Next, cut the figures out with the help of a grownup and paint them any way you like best. Here we suggest several ideas, but the part that is the most fun is to let your imagination fly and create your own designs!

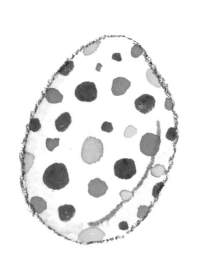

Another great idea is to draw masks of different animals and then add wings, ears, hands, and so on.

You may even use some cotton to make the bunny's hair!

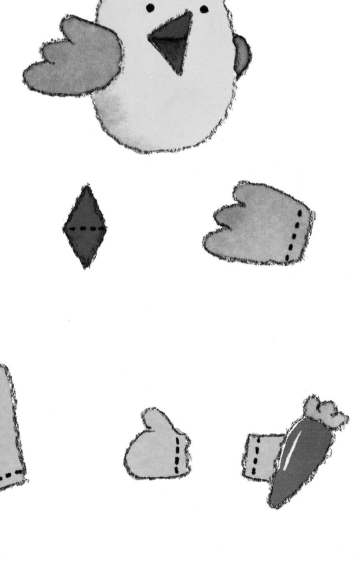

Guide for the parents

Spring

Spring starts March 21st and ends June 21st. These dates will allow you to play with a calendar; mark the beginning and the end of the season as well as the date of all the holidays in spring. It is a good way to start learning the months.

Trees in bloom

Almond trees and cherry trees, like all trees, have roots, trunks, branches, and leaves. They bloom in spring and each almond or cherry blossom becomes a fruit. The fruit has a seed inside (the little round pit in cherries and the kernel in almonds). If we plant the seed, a little plant will be born and over time it will grow and become another almond (or cherry) tree.

Nests

Swallows make their nests mixing mud with saliva. They use protected corners in buildings to make them. The male and female swallow mate and lay eggs. When baby swallows come out of the egg, their parents feed them until they grow up and they all stay together until summer is over; that is when their long trip begins. The following spring they always come back to the same nest, the one they abandoned in the fall.

Plants grow and leaves sprout

Rivers are full of water from the snow that melts up in the mountains. It rains quite a bit and it gets warmer. This allows the world to grow green again: the first leaves sprout from the trees, flowers bloom, and all plants grow. This abundance means there is a lot of food for animals. It is a season full of life.

Unsteady weather

Spring is a season when the weather is usually quite unsteady. A good way to awaken an interest for observation in children is to have them pay attention to the weather in one week. If the children are learning how to write, it is a good time to ask them to write about the weather instead of drawing what it is like. Any excuse is a good one to have them practice reading and writing. Draw a square and include all the days of the week with room on the side to write or draw what the weather is like. If they like this exercise, go ahead and repeat it.

Tadpoles

Frogs lay their eggs in the spring. A few weeks later tiny tadpoles are born. After some time they lose their tails, grow legs, and become frogs. The warmer the water, the faster this transformation occurs.

	Monday	Tuesday	Wednesday	Thursday	Friday	Saturday	Sunday

Original book title in Catalan: *La Primavera*
© Copyright Gemser Publications S.L., 2004.
C/Castell, 38; Teià (08329) Barcelona, Spain (World Rights)
Tel: 93 540 13 53
E-mail: *info@mercedesros.com*
Author: Núria Roca
Illustrator: Rosa Maria Curto

First edition for the United States and Canada (exclusive rights), and the rest of the world (non-exclusive rights) published in 2004 by Barron's Educational Series, Inc.

Address all inquiries to:
Barron's Educational Series, Inc.
250 Wireless Boulevard
Hauppauge, New York 11788
http://www.barronseduc.com

International Standard Book Number 0-7641-2733-0
Library of Congress Catalog Card Number 2004101341

Printed in Spain
9 8 7 6 5 4 3 2 1

THE SEASONS

Spring